The Sky ⌐

Written and illustrated by Annalisa Jackson

To Mikayla Mae

I hope you always find rainbows

Annalisa

Jack

For my beloved Nan who I see when the rainbows shine. And for my Mum, for always believing in me. Love always Lise.

There was a time when a rain cloud grew very sad.

He was a young cloud, only small, and had not shed his rain many times.

But each time he rained he listened to the people on the

ground below and it would
make him sad.

"Rain, rain go away!"
"When is this rain going to
stop?"

"Oh no its raining AGAIN!"

"I wish the sun would come and chase this rain away!" The little cloud wished he brought people happiness and joy like the sun did.

So he decided to go and visit the sun to ask his advice.

The sun was busy drying puddles when the cloud came over. His smile was warm and gentle.

"Oh Mr Sun" the small cloud said, "Please tell me how to make people happy like you do. I'm so fed up of making people sad.

The sun turned and smiled at the little cloud. "I cannot tell you how I make people happy. I just smile and they smile too."

The little cloud shook his head. "But, Mr Sun, how can I make people smile?"

The sun thought for a moment. "Go to see the Sky Painter little one. She put you here, and I. If anyone can answer your question it is her."

The little cloud thanked the sun and floated away in search of the Sky Painter.

He eventually found her near a clear, blue patch of sky. All around her feet were pots of coloured paint and brushes. She was stood, deep in thought, staring at the sky.

The little cloud moved towards her slowly. "Excuse me Sky Painter", he said softly.

The Sky Painter turned and smiled a slow, kind smile at the little cloud. Her deep blue eyes twinkled. "Yes little one?" she said.

The little cloud felt happy the Sky Painter could help him, and asked "Please tell me Sky Painter, how I can make people happy when I rain. It makes me so sad to hear them complain about my rain".

The Sky Painter picked her brush up and said, "Little one I must finish this painting. While I do why don't you look down at the ground again, and watch the people a little longer." She started to paint slowly and the little cloud floated away feeling sad.

When the little cloud had floated off a little he looked down and he saw a gardener digging in his garden.

"Thank goodness it rained today" the gardener said. "My

flowers needed the water so badly". And the gardener smiled.

The cloud felt a little less sad and turned around to speak to the Sky Painter. But she was still painting, "Watch a bit longer little one", she said as she painted.

This time the little cloud floated in a different direction, and stopped at a park. In the park were young children in rain coats and wellies.

As the little cloud watched the children smiled and laughed, and danced in his puddles. The little cloud smiled in delight at their happiness.

This time he did not turn back to the Sky Painter but carried on watching.

He floated a bit further and saw people in other countries who had no water to drink.

They were filling up their drinking containers at the river, that had water now that it had rained. They drank the water and smiled.

The little cloud floated back to the Sky Painter.

"I think I understand now Sky Painter", he said. "I cannot make everybody smile the way the sun does. But every bit of joy that comes from my rain is special, and I will look harder next time".

The Sky Painter turned around and smiled too. "You are right my little friend. People will not always be happy, but it is important to enjoy every moment of happiness.

Look at my new painting".

The little cloud turned and saw a beautiful rainbow soaring over the clear blue sky.
"Rainbows will only come when there is rain AND sun" the Sky Painter said.

"I put them here to remind everyone that the rain is as important as the sun, and only after the rain has come will you see such a lovely thing as this, while you stand in the sun's smile".

The little cloud thanked the Sky Painter, and he was never sad about having to rain again.

Every time he saw a rainbow he remembered how important he was.

AJ.

44871375R00016

Printed in Poland
by Amazon Fulfillment
Poland Sp. z o.o., Wrocław